For Aunt Dee and Uncle Paul
and their delightful tribe
J.H.

To Amelia,
with thanks
I.B.

First published 2002 by Walker Books Ltd
87 Vauxhall Walk, London SE11 5HJ

This edition published 2003

10 9 8 7 6 5 4 3 2

Text © 2002 Judy Hindley
Illustrations © 2002 Ivan Bates

This book has been typeset in
Stempel Schneidler and Metropolis

Printed in China

British Library Cataloguing in Publication Data:
a catalogue record for this book
is available from the British Library

ISBN 0-7445-9480-4

THIS WALKER BOOK BELONGS TO:

_____

_____

_____

_____

Do
Like
a Duck
Does!

JUDY HINDLEY

illustrated by

IVAN BATES

WALKER BOOKS
AND SUBSIDIARIES
LONDON • BOSTON • SYDNEY

Five little ducklings,
following their
mother –

whatever
any duck does,
so does every other.

So they waddle and they hop
and they scuttle and they stop –

Flop! Flop! Flop! Flop! Flop!

All together.

"**Quack!**" says Mama Duck,

"That's the way to be!

Do like a duck does!

Do like me!"

There go the ducklings, all in a line.
But who's creep-creeping close, following behind?

"Wait!" says Mama, "You don't belong with us!
Stop!" says Mama, "Do you think you're a duck?"

"But of course!" says the stranger, with a waddle and a strut. "That's just what I am — a big, brown duck."

Well, he has no feathers
and he has no beak.
He has four claws
on his hairy-scary feet.
He has two ears
that stick up a mile,
and a wicked
foxy nose and
a wicked
foxy smile.

But Mama says, "Well, then, do like us.
Head up, tail up, toes pointing out.
Stretch your little wings, dear,
straighten up your back.
Do like a duck does –

**Quack!
Quack!
Quack!"**

So Mama leads
them off together –

Hup! Hup! Hup!

Five little ducklings and a big brown duck –
a hairy-scary stranger ... a very silly duck!

"Look!" says Mama.
"What a lovely patch of muck!
Jump in the puddle, dear.
Show you're a duck!
Lots of bugs and beetles
swimming in the scum.
Open up your beak, dear.

**Yum!
Yum!
Yum!"**

Now the very hairy stranger
has some notions of his own,
and he's looking
at the ducklings
when he says,

**"Yum,
yum..."**

And he's creeping
ever closer … and
he's very,
very
near…

But Mama turns and catches him,
and says, "Look here!
You don't like bugs.
You don't like muck.
You can't say quack…
Are you *sure*
you're a duck?"

"Yes, I am!"
says the stranger.
"It's really, really true!

I can waddle.
I can scuttle.
I can strut a little, too.

I'm a duck!
I'm a duck!
I'm a duck like you!"

So Mama says,
"Show it! Prove you're a duck.
Do like a duck does! Do like us!"
Then they zip through the thistles and ...

they slip into the river – **Plop! Plop! Plop!**

Plop! Plop! All together.

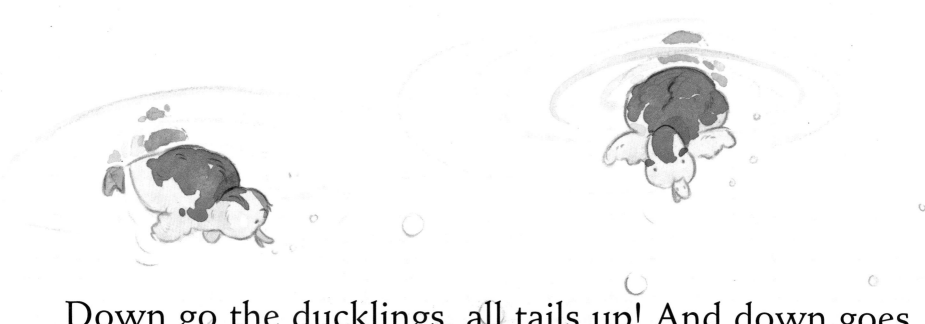

Down go the ducklings, all tails up! And down goes

the stranger – **Glup! Glup! Glup!**

So where are all the ducklings now?
Here they all come – **Pop!**

Pop! Pop! Pop! Pop! Every one.

But where's the
very hairy-scary stranger?

Gone home.

"Well," says Mama.
"What a bit of luck!

But I always really knew ...
that was no duck!"